Pout-Pout Fish

Pout-Pout Fish Back to School

Written by **Wes Adams**   Illustrated by **Isidre Monés**

Based on the *New York Times*–bestselling Pout-Pout Fish books
written by Deborah Diesen and illustrated by Dan Hanna

Farrar Straus Giroux
New York

Farrar Straus Giroux Books for Young Readers
An imprint of Macmillan Publishing Group, LLC
175 Fifth Avenue, New York, NY 10010

Color separations by Embassy Graphics
Printed in China by RR Donnelley Asia Printing Solutions Ltd., Dongguan City, Guangdong Province
Designed by Aram Kim
First edition, 2019
10 9 8 7 6 5 4 3 2 1

mackids.com

Library of Congress Control Number: 2018955246
ISBN: 978-0-374-31047-9

Our books may be purchased in bulk for promotional, educational, or business use.
Please contact your local bookseller or the Macmillan Corporate and Premium Sales Department at
(800) 221-7945 ext. 5442 or by email at MacmillanSpecialMarkets@macmillan.com.

It was a big day for Mr. Fish. He was going back to school.

Mr. Fish was going to be a substitute teacher—for the very first time. Poor Miss Hewitt was home with a cold. She had been Mr. Fish's favorite teacher when he was a small fry.

As he said goodbye to his Snoozy Snuggly and scooted out the door, he tried not to worry about his new job.

Swimming up to the entrance, he met a nervous little fish who was just starting school.

"Welcome!" said Pout-Pout Fish. "This is my first day as a teacher. We will have to help each other today."

Inside, students were darting left and right. The little fry felt lost.

Mr. Fish remembered where to go.
"Follow me!" he said.

In the classroom, the little fry was welcomed by the other students.

But at the front of the class, their substitue teacher was nervous and felt like clamming up.

The little fry raised a fin. "Can you tell us about when you were a kinderguppy like us?" he asked Mr. Fish.

Mr. Fish remembered lots
of stories that made
the students laugh.

It was a good start to a busy morning.

At lunchtime, all the fish went to get their lunch boxes.
The little fry discovered he'd forgotten his.
"Don't fret," said Mr. Fish. "You can share with me."

At recess, the little fry was relieved when the other students asked him to play. But he thought Pout-Pout Fish looked lonely.

"Follow me!" the little fish said to his teacher.

On the playground, Mr. Fish taught the students a new game. They leaped and soared, dodged and ducked.

Back in the classroom, a weary Mr. Fish was ready for Rest Period.

Some students napped. The little fry worked quietly at his desk.

Soon it was time to pack up and go home. The little fry gave Mr. Fish a beautiful drawing. And the whole class had one thing to say to their wonderful substitute teacher.

"THANK YOU, POUT-POUT FISH!"

Turn little pouts into big smiles with
this paperback series based on
the *New York Times*-bestselling books.

Two pages of
stickers included!

Pout-Pout Fish is going back
to school—as a substitute teacher!
He feels nervous . . . that is, until he meets
a new little fry with his own first-day jitters.

There are more
Pout-Pout Fish books
in the sea.

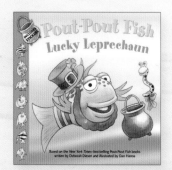

For more fishy fun, visit
poutpoutfish.com.

US $5.99 / CAN $7.99
ISBN 978-0-374-31047-9